Mother,
There Is a Mouse
in This House

By
Doris J. Finch

Print information available on the last page

Rev. date: 06/08/2016

To order additional copies of this book, contact:
Xlibris
1-888-795-4274
www.Xlibris.com
Orders@Xlibris.com

Mother,
There Is a Mouse
in This House

By
Doris J. Finch

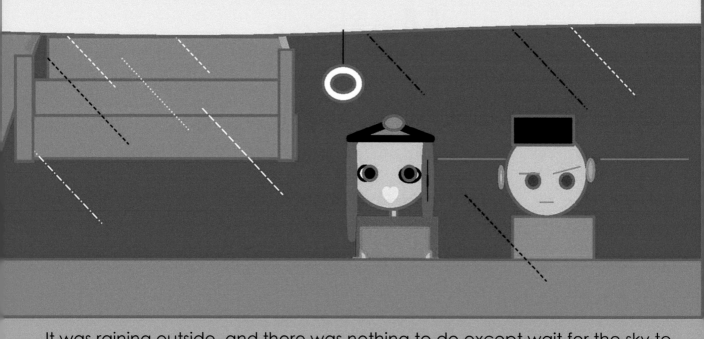

It was raining outside, and there was nothing to do except wait for the sky to turn from black back to blue.

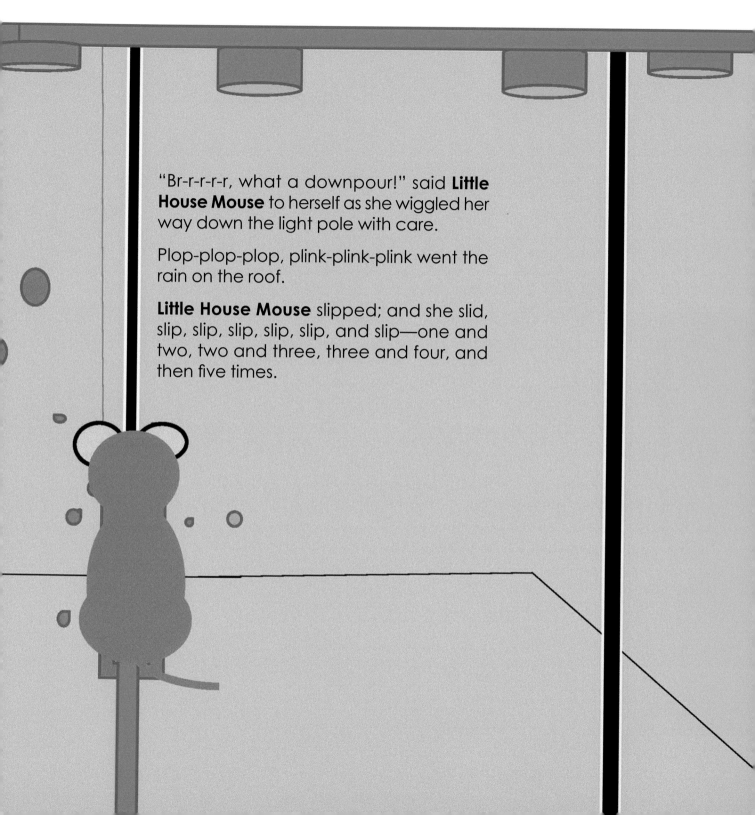

"Br-r-r-r, what a downpour!" said **Little House Mouse** to herself as she wiggled her way down the light pole with care.

Plop-plop-plop, plink-plink-plink went the rain on the roof.

Little House Mouse slipped; and she slid, slip, slip, slip, slip, slip, and slip—one and two, two and three, three and four, and then five times.

Little House Mouse was on the move, running and skipping, around the big room.

What fun! thought **Little House Mouse** as she scurried about. And while she was not looking—Whack! Bum-pi-ty bump into the side of the wall she thumped. *Hum-m-m, a very short wall it was,* she thought.

Up, up, up; creep, creep, creep; up the slippery side, sharp nails scratching and clinging to hang on. Creepy creep, creep; wobble, wobble; around the edge until splat down from the top she tumbled.

"Eek, eek, e-e-k, e-e-k!" she squeaked, moving around, feeling for something that did not hurt her furry hide.

Inside, a magician's wand and curtain rods had poked her and prod her, and then she felt what was silk, a net, and some clothing. There was a needle and thread and a ball of yarn. A set of bells did jingle and jangle. Jing-a-ling, ting-a-ling, a pleasing bell tune. But its song was not enough to stop **Little House Mouse** from crying.

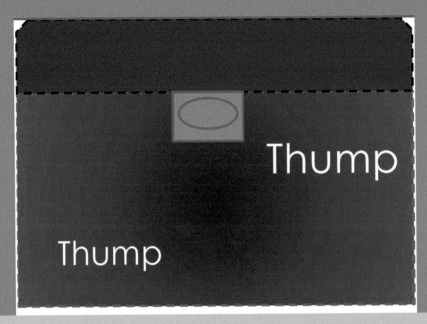

Thump

Thump

Little House Mouse cried her tears until they were all but dried up as the clock on the wall played tick-tock, tick-tock, tick-tock. Soon **Little House Mouse** fell into an uneasy sleep, and she began to dream.

In her dream, a mouse was trapped inside a large empty container. And she was running around inside, saying, "I will never give up, I will never give up, never give up."

Little House Mouse tossed and she turned as the mouse's words played over and over again inside her dream. Soon after, **Little House Mouse** woke up and found that she was still inside her prison of a box with all the odds and ends that had poked and did prod her. Feeling all alone, **Little House Mouse** began touching the things inside the box. She was searching for anything that would help her to get out of the prison of a box. Thinking back to the mouse in her dream, **Little House Mouse** began to think of ways to break free of the box. All of a sudden, her eyes grew bright, and her lips widened into a smile. Then these words tumbled out from her happy mousey smile: "I will dress myself up so that no one would know me, then bring down the roof on this house if I have to."

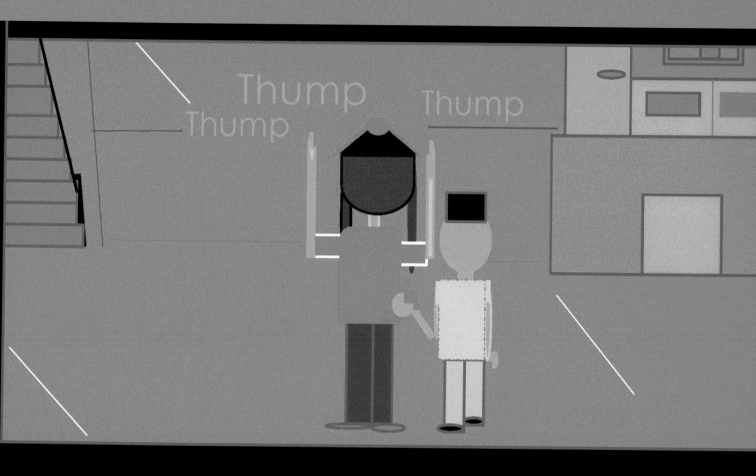

Peg and then Tim had heard thump, thump, thump, and thump. Then the two housebound kids had turned left and then right then north but not south because the noise had grown louder. Thump, thump, thump, thump, thump, and thump, thump!

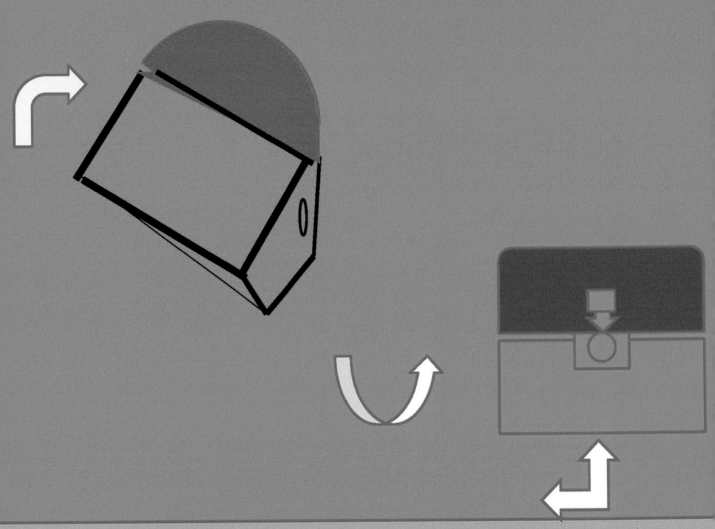

Up the stairs, the two went but not in a hurry. What a sight the two made, looking afraid of their shadows.

Thump, thump and jump and jump went the trunk with the junk. It almost spilled over with all the stuff.

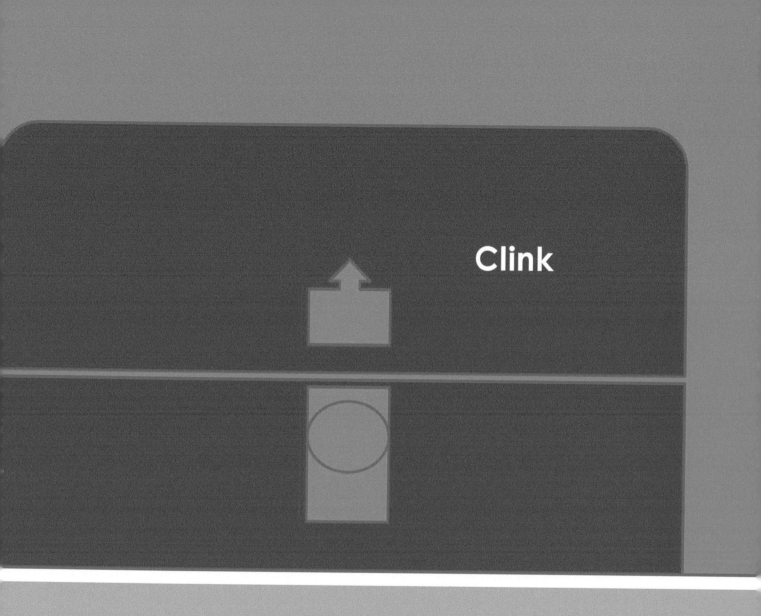

Little House Mouse could hear whispers then clink and then clink. And from the deep end of the trunk, she called on all her strength, and she counted aloud, "One, two," and then "three."

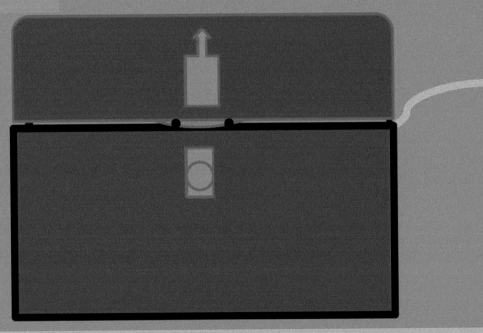

And it had took all her nerve, but with her two eyes opened wide and in her wee tiny voice that was not more than a squeak, she said, "It is me it is me, the Tooth Fairy."

And with the battery pack that had come with the wings,
she arose from the trunk in spite of all the things.

And with the flick of her wings, she did rise up, up, up, up. And she held on to the air near the trap of a trunk.

"Welcome, Tooth Fairy. This is Peg, and I am Tim. We are most happy to meet you, and we want to be your friends."

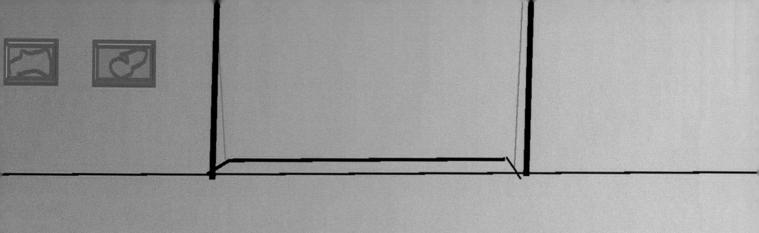

Down the stairs the two went with the Tooth Fairy overhead. She was fluttering her wings and hiding her fangs.

And she started to sing a happy tune that went like this: "Zee yippee ding-ding, zing-zing zippy ya-ya. Wee zippy da-da-da mee tippy da-da."

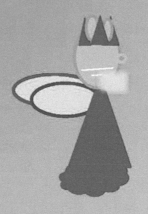

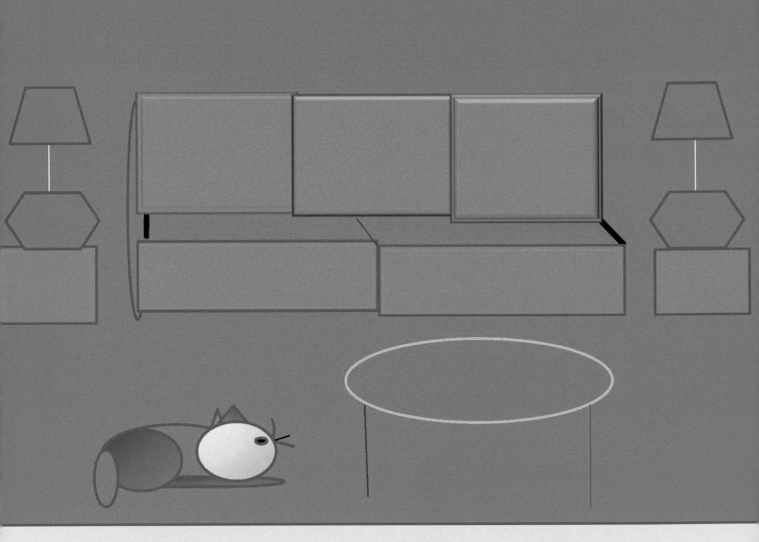

Down the stairs the three went. They were joking and laughing.

"Come, my friends," said the Tooth Fairy in her squeak of a voice. "Let us break with some supper. Cheese, if you please, for this weary Tooth Fairy."

Little House Mouse really was hungry, and her tummy was growling. But neither of the friends were aware of one thing—that being Tiger, the cat. She was watching the three of them.

Again, **Little House Mouse** sang out, and she was putting on airs. And Tiger had been awakened, feeling grouchy from her short nap. Tiger raised her head, and her nose started to twitch. Her whiskers fanned out and took in the air. Her nose went to sniffing and twitching in the air as if something was fishy or had soured the clean air. And being the mad cat that she was, she struck out at the air, tearing away until a scratch of a paw caught what she had caught. The sharp paw grabbed the pink of a gown, and the ripping of the gown was an awful frightful sound.

R-r-r-
r-r-i-
i-i-p-
p-p

The gown ripped from her torso, and the wings started to fail. They sputtered and sputtered until the battery went dead. And anyone could see that this tiny little thing was more than it appeared at the beginning of things. The children were shocked, and they started to stare when, suddenly, the veil, it fluttered down in the air. And the children could see **Little House Mouse** hanging there with broken wings, bucked toothed, and exposed to the pair. And what was even worse, she could not hold on to the air.

Down she went to the floor with a splat. And do you know what she looked like uncovered like that? **Little House Mouse** looked like a fake of a Tooth Fairy falling down from the air. And it was with no further ado that she started to backtrack. Up, up she had went, seeing the meddling cat.

"Why?" asked Tim, looking a wee bit upset. Because he had started to care about the tiny fairy like she was his very own pet.

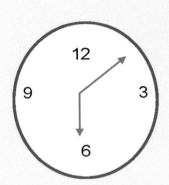

Peg peeked upstairs and back again at her little brother. And they looked and they looked from one to the other.

Tim asked of Peg, "Why did the Tooth Fairy run away?"

Peg being Peg did not really want to say. Instead, Peg said to Tim that the Tooth Fairy would come back to see them one day. And when Tim had started to act like himself again, Peg thought about how fast the Tooth Fairy ran. And not too much later, to her mother she said, "there is a mouse in this house and it is a little show off."

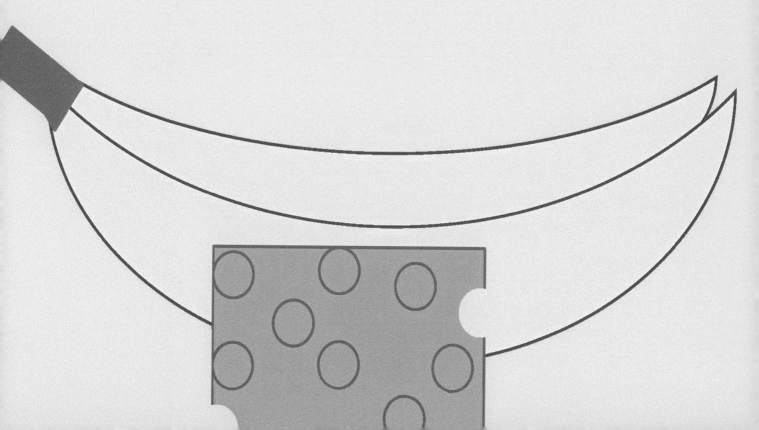

Printed in the United States
By Bookmasters